Chance Lincoln,
Boy Detective

Chance Lincoln, Boy Detective

Can You Solve the Mysteries?

Shane Fortune

Edited by Carol Ann A. Fortune

Book Cover Illustrations by Christian Fortune

Dedication

For my mom, *Jackie*

Table of Contents

Other Great Books by the Author

Chance Lincoln, Everyone Needs a Second Chance

Chance Lincoln, Around the World

Nick and Myron's Double Diary
Discover the misadventures of two sixth-grade misfits who stumble through life without a clue.

<u>Preface</u>

The solution to each case is located in the back portion of this book, beginning on page 128—immediately following the epilogue.

The Chance Challenge— Are You Ready?

Are you ready to take the Chance Challenge? The adventures of Chance Lincoln are fun to read, but even more fun to read out loud to a friend. Most people can't read a Chance story out loud without stumbling over the words. *Can you?*

Do you feel like a challenge? Then *Take a Chance!*

The Case of the Jewelry Janitor

Ted Lincoln, a young police officer, heard the banging of a hammer as he quickly walked up the driveway to his Cousin Chance's workshop.

"Ow! Watch what you're doing, Louie!" Ted heard Chance shout from within.

"Sorry," replied another voice. "It was an accident."

"Give me the hammer! This time *you* hold the nail," demanded Chance.

The sign on the workshop door read,

Chance Lincoln
Detective Agency
(And Dog Waste Removal)
Take a Chance
Only $5

Inside, Chance, an 11-year-old boy, and his friend, Lucky Louie, were building something out of wood. Messy piles of shattered lumber were strewn randomly across the floor. Chance's right thumb was throbbing red from the hammer hit he took from Louie a moment ago. Now a very nervous Louie was holding the nail. Chance drew back the hammer for a mighty blow.

"Don't miss," pleaded Louie.

"Don't worry," answered Chance, as he furrowed his brow in concentration. "I never miss."

"Hi, Cousin Chance," interrupted Ted as he threw open the door.

"Oh! Hi, Cousin Ted!" replied a surprised Chance as he slammed the hammer down.

"Ow!" shouted Lucky Louie. "You said you never missed!"

"Sorry, Louie!"

Ted raised a disapproving eyebrow as he looked around the cluttered room. He saw sawdust, wood chips, rusty bent nails, and wet paint splotches scattered everywhere. Ted hoped none of this disaster would get on his perfectly pressed uniform.

"Did a hurricane hit your workshop?" Ted asked as he opened a window to let in some fresh air. It made the shop smell worse. He looked out the window and saw three garbage cans underneath it. Whatever was in them, a cloud of flies loved it. Ted closed the window.

"We're building a go-cart," answered Chance.

"You know," Ted said sarcastically, "go-carts run a lot better if they're not made of splinters."

"Yes," said Chance, embarrassed. "We're just getting started."

"I'd hate to see this place when you're done," Ted continued. Ted felt something gooey on his hands.

He looked at his hands and said, "Chance, why is there red paint on my hands?"

"Because you opened the window before the paint dried," Chance answered. "Louie, I thought I asked you to put up the *Wet Paint* sign."

"I told you I'd do it later," answered Louie.

"When?" snapped Chance. "After the paint dries?"

Ted grabbed a filthy rag and wiped his hands with it. Now he had four types of paint on them.

"Chance," Ted said, "I need your help right away."

"Is your dog sick again? I'll come over just as soon as I grab my gloves and carpet cleanser."

"No," replied Ted. "The dog and the carpet are fine. It's Jack Jenkins."

"*Old Man* Jenkins?" asked Chance.

"No, his son Jack Jenkins, Junior—the one who used to be a champion high-jumper at Jersey Junior College."

"Better known as Jumping-Jack Jenkins?"

"The same," Ted assured.

"Didn't Jumping-Jack do jumping-jacks at Jim's Gym?" asked Chance.

"Yes. But Jumping-Jack invented a special kind of jumping-jack for jittery jumpers," Ted said.

"What were they called?"

"Jumping-Jack's jumping-jacks," smiled Ted.

"I thought Jumping-Jack Jenkins was in Jersey Jail?" Chance asked.

"He was," answered Ted, "for carjacking. But when he got out, he jettisoned his life of crime and became a janitor."

"Where?"

"Jazmyn's Jewelry Shop," Ted replied.

"Expensive jewelry?" inquired Chance.

"Yes, the finest from Germany."

"But who would hire a jailbird to be a jewelry janitor?"

"Old Lady Jazmyn, the Jewelry Queen. She felt sorry for Jumping-Jack Jenkins, so she gave him a job. But now she feels jilted."

"Why?" Chance asked.

"Her jewelry store was robbed," Ted explained. "All her gems, jewelry, and jellybean jars were stolen."

"So Jazmyn thinks that Janitor Jumping-Jack Jenkins, Junior, the jailbird, jacked her German jewels?"

"Just so! But I think he's innocent. Will you take the case?"

"Of course," smiled Chance. "It sounds juicy."

Ted parked the police car in front of Jazmyn's Jewelry Shop. It was a beautiful sunny day.

Ted stopped as they came up to the store. Chance could see their clear reflections. Ted, who was always fussy about how he looked, used the reflection to comb his hair and adjust his hat. He smiled at his mirror image.

"Hello, handsome," he purred. "The girls are sure lucky you're around!"

Chance rolled his eyes in disbelief.

"Is anybody in the store, yet?" Chance asked.

Ted squinted at the window. "I don't know," Ted answered. "I can only see myself." Then he smiled again. "Of course, that's plenty." Ted winked at himself.

"Why do the windows reflect like that?"

"Many stores have windows that are made to reflect sunrays to help keep the stores cool. If customers get too hot, they'll stop shopping and leave."

Just then, Ms. Jazmyn drove into the parking lot, got out of her car, and unlocked the door.

"Come on in, boys," she said as she turned on the lights.

"It's a shame about Janitor Jenkins," she continued. "I quite liked him. He was pleasant and kept the building in good order."

"What," Chance asked, "makes you so sure that Jack Jenkins was the one who stole from you?"

"Dearie," she answered gently, "there was a witness. My store manager, Mr. Motley, saw the whole thing. Here he comes now."

"Mr. Motley," asked Ted, "could you tell us what you saw?"

"Yes, Officer," Motley replied. "I live in the house directly across the street from here. The store was closed last Sunday. It was a beautiful day, like today, so I was working in my garden in my front yard when I thought I heard a noise from the store. I looked up and saw our janitor, Jack Jenkins, sneaking around in the store."

"Does Jenkins have keys to the store?" Chance asked.

"Of course," answered Mr. Motley.

"Does he normally clean the jewelry store on Sundays?" Ted asked.

"No," replied Mr. Motley. "That's what was so odd. He also left the lights off, as if he didn't want to be seen, as he sneaked around the dark store and put jewelry into a large bag. But the sun was so bright that I could clearly see his face."

Ted turned to Chance and sighed with despair. "This doesn't look good for Jenkins."

"Once a thief, always a thief," Mr. Motley said. "I told Ms. Jazmyn that hiring Jailbird Jenkins to be the janitor was a big mistake."

"No, Mr. Motley," responded Chance. "The only mistake she made was hiring *you*."

"What do you mean, young man?" asked Old Lady Jazmyn, surprised.

"I mean that Mr. Motley, in order to cover his own theft, is lying about seeing Jack Jenkins steal your jewelry."

How did Chance know that Mr. Motley was lying about seeing Jack Jenkins?

*(Turn to page **128** for the solution to **"The Case of the Jewelry Janitor."**)*

<u>The Case of the Purple Puppies</u>

A forty-year-old woman walked up the driveway to Chance's workshop. Just then, she saw Chance Lincoln and Lucky Louie pushing a go-cart out of the workshop and onto the street. A long electrical cord that was connected to the engine ran all the way back into a socket in the workshop.

"Boys, do you know where I can find Chance Lincoln?"

"Right here, Ma'am," Chance answered as he waved at her. "I'll be with you in a minute."

"What are you doing, young man?" she asked.

"We're testing our new go-cart: the All-electric, Turbo-powered, Supersonic X1-11-GC. The GC stands for *Go-Cart*."

"But first," added Louie, "we have to decide who's going to test drive it."

"And there's only one way to do that," said Chance. "Ready, Louie?"

"Rock-Paper-Scissors!" they both yelled.

"You win, Louie," Chance said. "No wonder they call you *Lucky*."

"And I feel lucky today," Louie laughed as he put on his racing helmet.

Chance waved a checkered racing flag as he yelled into a bullhorn.

"Driver," he yelled, "start your engine!"

Lucky Louie revved up his engine. ***VROOM! VROOM! VROOM!***

A cranky old man hurried out of the house next door.

"Chance!" he yelled angrily. "What's that *awful* noise?"

"Oh, hi, Mr. Hannigan!" Chance shouted through the bullhorn, making Mr. Hannigan wish he had turned off his hearing aids. "We're testing our new go-cart!"

"No, Chance! Not here!"

But it was too late. Chance waved the flag down and yelled, "Go!"

Louie stomped on the pedal. The go-cart raced forward.

VROOM! SCREECH! PHHHTTT! CRASH!

Lucky Louie and the go-cart knocked down Mr. Hannigan's overloaded trash cans like a bowling ball. Garbage sprayed everywhere, and last week's banana-cream pie splattered all over Mr. Hannigan.

Mr. Hannigan wiped the pie from his eyes. "Chance, you're a menace! In my day, you'd get a whooping, boy!"

"Sorry, Mr. Hannigan!" Chance responded as the old man went back inside his house.

Louie was filthy but not hurt.

"What happened, Chance?" he asked.

"The go-cart ran out of extension cord. When it did, the cord tugged on the cart and made it spin out into the trash cans."

The visiting woman explained her problem to Chance as the boys picked up the trash.

"My name is Paula Polly Paulson," she began.

"Try saying *that* ten times fast," cracked Louie to Chance.

"Quiet, Louie, and pick up your mess!" Chance replied.

"Pleased to meet you, Ms. Paulson," Chance continued. "What's the problem?"

"I raise and train puppies."

"Are your puppies popular?" Chance chimed.

"Yes," insisted Paula. "And very precious."

"Why?"

"Because the puppies are purple. I raise the world's only purple puppies."

"What happened?"

"Someone pinched my whole pack of purple puppies."

"You mean they were stolen?" Chance asked.

"Yes, that's what I said," Paula persisted. "They were pinched."

"Do you suspect anyone in particular?"

"Yes, my old rival, Pippy Piper, the puppy pincher."

"Pippy Piper pinched a pack of purple puppies?"

"Yes! A pack of purple puppies Pippy Piper pinched."

"But if Pippy Piper pinched a pack of purple puppies, where's the pack of purple puppies Pippy Piper pinched?"

"Precisely! That's what I'd like to know!" Paula said.

"What about the police?" Chance asked.

"They can't do anything, because I have no proof. Chance," Paula pleaded, "can you prove that Pippy Piper pinched my pack of purple puppies?"

"Probably."

"Perfect!"

Chance and Ted went to Pippy's house. Lucky Louie joined them.

"I had nothing to do with the puppy theft," Pippy insisted. "I wasn't even in the country at the time."

"Where were you?" Ted asked.

"I was in Antarctica," she answered.

"Where is Antarctica, Chance?" Louie asked.

"It's on the bottom of the globe. It's always covered in ice and snow."

"Oh," said Louie. "So it's like the North Pole, except everyone stands upside down."

"Be quiet, Louie."

"What were you doing in Antarctica, Ms. Piper?" Ted continued.

"I was taking pictures of penguins playing with each other," Pippy replied.

"What were they playing? Freeze Tag?" giggled Louie.

"Very funny," Chance said. "Now zip it."

Pippy continued, "I also saw some polar bears. They were magnificent! I'll never forget my trip to Antarctica!"

"I'll bet," agreed Chance. "It's impossible to forget a trip which you never made. You were never in Antarctica."

How did Chance know that Pippy was never in Antarctica?

*(Turn to page **129** for the solution to "**The Case of the Purple Puppies**.")*

The Case of the Silver Caesar

An older woman dressed in black walked up the driveway to Chance's workshop. She bumped into a redheaded boy with freckles. His face was covered in soot, and he was carrying a small fire extinguisher.

"Sorry, ma'am," the boy said.

"Hello," said the woman. "I'm Mrs. Nellie Nelson from New York, New York."

"And I'm Lucky Louie from Walla Walla," giggled the boy.

"What happened to your face?"

Lucky Louie wiped some of the soot from around his eyes and

stared at the soot on his fingers. "Mice," laughed Louie.

"Mice?"

"Mice. They're little trouble-makers," Louie smiled.

Just then, Mr. Hannigan came out on his porch, coughing and shaking his fist.

"Louie!" the old man yelled. "You tell Chance that this smoke is ruining my barbeque! You tell him that I'm going to call the fire department and tell them NOT to come, so his workshop will burn to the ground!"

"*Who* was that?" Nellie asked.

"That's our friend, Mr. Hannigan."

"Your *friend?* He sure looks angry."

"Yeah," chuckled Louie, "that's why we call him 'Heart-Attack Harry.' But he'll be all right. He just needs to take his medicine."

"Where can I find Chance Lincoln?" Nellie asked.

"He's in his workshop," Lucky Louie answered. "Just follow the smoke."

Nellie poked her head through the open doorway. She saw a boy wearing a gas mask. He was spraying the contents of his fire extinguisher onto a smoking go-cart.

"WHAT ON EARTH HAPPENED HERE?" Nellie exclaimed.

"Mice," the boy answered. "Never trust them!"

"Mice set your go-cart on fire?"

"They sure did. They ate right through the power cord while the go-cart was plugged-in, and that started an electrical fire. *And after all that cheese we fed them!* Little backstabbers!"

"Where can I find Chance Lincoln?"

The boy looked at her through his gas mask.

"You're looking at him."

Chance continued spraying the smoking go-cart.

"Maybe I should come back when things are normal."

"This *is* normal."

Now that the fire was extinguished, Chance opened a window and pulled off his gas mask.

Nellie stared at Chance suspiciously. "Are you sure you're a detective?"

"The best one you'll ever meet in this workshop," Chance said with a grin.

"I'm Mrs. Nellie Nelson, from the New York, New York, Musty Museum of Moldy Marvels and Really Old Stuff."

"Pleased to meet you," Chance replied.

"Ms. Jazmyn, whom you helped earlier, is an old friend of mine. She recommended you."

"What seems to be the problem?"

"Two teenage boys in your town claim to have found a valuable coin, and they are offering to sell it to the museum for a small fortune."

"What type of coin is it?"

"It's a silver Caesar," Nellie answered.

"A silver coin with an image of Caesar on the front?" Chance asked.

"Exactly!" Nellie continued. "But what makes this silver Caesar so shocking is where it was found."

"Where was it found?"

"Right here!"

"Right here?"

"Yes, right here off the West Coast of America!"

"Really?" Chance asked.

"Yes!" continued Nellie. "If this coin was really found here, then that means that the Ancient Romans came to America fifteen hundred years before Columbus! They may even have been the first people to sail around the world!"

"Wow!" said Chance.

"Naturally, the Musty Museum is very excited to obtain this coin."

"Tell me," Chance asked, "how much would this coin be worth if it had been found in Rome, instead of America?"

"Oh, very little," Nellie replied. "Lots of Roman coins have been found in Rome."

"How did you learn about this coin?"

"Well," Nellie recalled, "two brothers, named Shel and Seymour Sosser, called my supervisor, Shirley Shilly. They said they spotted the silver Caesar when they went diving for seashells."

"I see," said Chance.

"The silver Caesar sighting caused a great stir, but Shirley Shilly wants to be sure that the Sosser's aren't just selling us a silly story. That would be shabby."

"Surely!" Then Chance asked, "Do the Sosser siblings have any witnesses?"

"Yes. Sheila Seltzer said she saw the Sosser's find the silver Caesar while she was selling."

"You mean, 'sailing?'"

"No, I mean 'selling.' Sheila sells seashells by the seashore."

"But did she see Shel and Seymour explore the seafloor?"

"Yes, and Sheila saw Shel and Seymour swim ashore to Sherry's Shoe Store."

"Really? Why did they swim to the shoe store?"

"Shoes were half off."

"That would do it."

"Chance, will you see if the Sosser's story is sincere?"

"Certainly."

Nellie, Chance, and Lucky Louie went to the place on the beach where Sheila sold seashells by the seashore.

"Okay, Mrs. Nelson. We're going to test the Sosser's story. Louie, you dive to the seafloor while I watch."

"I don't want to dive in. The water's cold," Louie protested.

"Oh, all right, Louie. Have it your way. *I'll* watch while *you* dive in."

"That's better! Hey! What are you trying to pull?"

"Okay, Louie. We'll play Rock-Paper-Scissors."

"Sounds fair."

"Rock-Paper-Scissors!" they both chanted as they played.

"You win, Louie, so you have to go in," Chance said.

"Dang," Louie replied as he dove into the water.

Chance could clearly see Louie touch the seafloor.

"So," Nellie said, "the Sosser's story *could* be true."

Nellie, Chance, and Louie paid a visit to the Sosser's treehouse.

"Here's the silver Caesar," said Shel. "Now, where's the money?"

"I'm writing you a check right now," Nellie answered.

"Just a moment," Chance said. "I'd like to see the coin."

The coin read, "Caesar 45 B.C."

"Forty-five B.C. was the year before Caesar died," explained Seymour. "So the coin is very, very old. It's worth a lot."

"Tear up your check, Mrs. Nelson," Chance warned. "This coin is a fake."

How did Chance know the coin was a fake?

(Turn to page **130** for the solution to *"The Case of the Silver Caesar."*)

The Case of the Buttermilk Biscuits

Mr. Harry Hannigan whistled happily as he weeded his tulips.

"What a perfect day," he thought to himself as he sipped his lemonade. "The sun is shining, the sky is blue, and, best of all, no Chance! Perfect."

Hannigan admired his colorful tulips. "Harry," he said to himself, "you're the world's greatest gardener!"

Hannigan smiled.

Then he frowned.

He heard the voices of Chance and Lucky Louie arguing with each other. Paradise perished.

Chance and Louie had pushed their go-cart onto the sidewalk, and it was pointed in the direction of his garden!

"Perfect!" he muttered to himself.

"But you got to drive the go-cart last time," protested Chance.

"But that's because I won at Rock-Paper-Scissors," Louie lectured. "If you want to drive it this time, you'll have to win again."

Hannigan looked up and saw two monsters disguised as innocent children. He knew that they were secretly plotting to destroy his tulips. Quick, where could he hide them? Nowhere, stupid; they were planted in his garden.

"Rock-Paper-Scissors!" the boys chanted as they played.

"I win!" shouted Chance gleefully. He strapped on the racing helmet.

Harry Hannigan was horrified.

"STOP!" he shouted. "Boys, what are you doing?"

"Oh, hi, Mr. Hannigan," Chance called cheerily. "We're testing our go-cart."

"I hoped–I mean–I thought it burned to ashes," Hannigan stated.

"Well, yes," Chance answered, "but this is a new one."

Hannigan admired the fact that Chance never quit. That's what he both loved and hated about Chance. But why couldn't some *other* old man admire Chance. Maybe he should sell his home and move to Florida. Life would be easier; he would only have to deal with hurricanes.

"Chance," he called out, "shouldn't you test drive your go-cart in the street?"

"We can't, Mr. Hannigan," Chance replied. "We're testing the brakes. If the brakes don't work, we could run into a car, and you know what that means, don't you?"

"I could enjoy some peace and quiet," Hannigan thought to himself. He didn't really mean it. He'd feel terrible if Chance got hurt–but he wouldn't feel much better if Chance ruined his tulips, either. Harry did some quick thinking.

"Chance," he sputtered, "you're right. It would be safer to test the brakes on the sidewalk, but why don't you turn your go-cart around so you won't run into my tulips?"

"Oooooh," said Chance. "That's a great idea, Mr. Hannigan! Louie, let's face this go-cart away from Mr. Hannigan's garden."

After the boys turned around the go-cart, Louie waved a checkered racing flag while yelling through a bullhorn. The bullhorn let out an irritating, high-pitched screech that reminded Hannigan of someone scratching a chalkboard with fingernails.

"Driver, start your engine," yelled Louie through the bullhorn.

"Why must they *yell* through a bullhorn," Hannigan thought to himself. "Bullhorns were invented so people wouldn't *need* to yell."

Chance revved the engine, *vroom, vroom, vroom!*

"Go!" shouted Louie.

VROOOOOOM!

The go-cart sped off in reverse! Mr. Hannigan jumped out of the way just in time as the go-cart slammed into his garden, sending tulip petals flying everywhere!

"Chance!" yelled Mr. Hannigan, "get that go-cart out of my garden this instant!"

"Right away!" obeyed Chance. But a rear tire got stuck in the soft soil, so when Chance stomped on the accelerator, all the go-cart did was rotate in a circle, destroying everything in its path and spraying dirt all over Mr. Hannigan.

"CHANCE LINCOLN! YOUR GO-CART HAS RUINED MY TULIPS!" shouted Heart-Attack Harry.

"Sorry, Mr. Hannigan!" Chance said sheepishly.

As Chance and Louie pushed the go-cart toward the workshop, Hannigan heard them talking to each other.

"Great news, Louie," Chance remarked. "The brakes work!"

"Yeah, Chance," commented Louie, "but we got to do something about those gears."

"We'll fix it tomorrow," Chance replied cheerfully.

Hannigan looked at his demolished garden. "Maybe I should learn to golf," he concluded.

A few moments later, a girl, about eight-years-old, walked into the workshop.

"I'm Betty Baxter; I live on Barker Street," said the little girl to Chance.

"Pleased to meet you, Betty," Chance replied.

Betty wiped away her tears and blew her nose into a blue handkerchief.

"I have a bit of a problem," Betty continued. "Do you know a boy by the name of Billy Barter?"

"Billy Barter, the bully of Barker Park?"

"That's him! The big jerk!"

"What did he do?"

"I baked a batch of buttermilk biscuits for my brothers—Bobby, Bradley, and Brady—but Billy Barter, the big bully, broke into my playhouse and stole them!"

"Did Billy, the bully, steal anything else?"

"Yes, he took a block of butter, a bucket of berries, and a bottle of my better batter."

"You mean, your 'best batter'?" corrected Chance.

"No, he didn't see the best batter," she answered. "It was at the bottom of a big, black box. He grabbed the 'better batter,' which is second best."

"A bitter story."

"You better believe it!" Betty bawled. "Chance, can you bring back my butter, berries, batter, and biscuits from that big bully, Billy Barter?"

"You bet!" Chance blurted.

"But, Chance, I don't have five dollars to pay you! All I have are three cents."

Chance looked at the sweet, little girl and smiled. "Oh, that's my *normal* price, Betty. But you're very lucky. I just happen to be having a three-cent sale for the next thirty seconds."

"Really?"

"You've got just twenty-five seconds left to pay me."

Betty panicked. "Here!" she yelled as she threw her three cents at Chance.

Chance was so surprised that he fell backward in his chair. But he laughed as he got up.

"I'll be back briskly," he said as he departed.

Chance banged on the backdoor of Billy Barter's blue clubhouse.

"What do you want?" Billy called out.

"I'm Chance Lincoln, and I've come to bring back Betty Baxter's buttermilk biscuits," Chance challenged.

"Well, you can't have them!" Billy, the bully, bellowed.

"Why not?" Chance asked.

Billy opened the door. "Because I didn't steal them. I traded for them."

"Betty says you stole them!"

"She's lying!" Billy Barter barked. "I traded Matt, my pet bat, for her butter, berries, batter, and biscuits! Betty's just bothered because Matt the Bat flew the coop."

"What?"

"She didn't put the bat in a cage, so he flew away," Billy explained. "I offered to sell her the cage the bat came in, but she didn't want to buy it. So now that Matt the Bat has made tracks, she wants her food back. She's just sore."

"What's that at the bottom of the cage, Billy?" Chance asked.

"Those are bat feathers," Billy explained. "Everyone knows that bats shed feathers this time of year."

"Hand over Betty's stuff, Billy," demanded Chance. "You made up the story about trading Matt the Bat for Betty's biscuits, and I can prove it!"

How does Chance know that Billy's story was untrue?

*(Turn to page **132** for the solution to "**The Case of the Buttermilk Biscuits**.")*

The Case of Sir Tristan's Talisman

Chance and Lucky Louie sucked on their peppermint sticks.

"I can't believe," Chance said, "that Mr. Hannigan gave us candy after we crashed our go-cart into the car in his driveway."

"He said that it was okay," said Louie, "because the car belongs to his brother-in-law. I don't know what that means."

"Me, neither," agreed Chance, "but I haven't seen Mr. Hannigan smile that big in years." said Chance.

At that moment, Ted Lincoln, dressed in his police uniform, burst through Chance's workshop door.

"Great news!" he exclaimed. "The Tri-City Museum has been robbed!"

Chance, baffled, stared at his cousin and blinked a few times in disbelief. Confused, Chance finally said awkwardly, "Congratulations?"

"Yeah," added Louie. "Maybe you'll get lucky, and tomorrow someone will rob the bank, too."

"You're a cop, Ted," Chance commented. "Why would a robbery make you happy?"

"Because the world famous Talisman of Sir Tristan has been stolen!"

"Never heard of it," mumbled Louie.

"This is a big case! So far, I've only worked small cases when other detectives have been sick or on vacation. If I can recover the Talisman, then I could be permanently promoted from traffic duty to the detective squad!"

Chance smiled. "That is wonderful news!" he said.

"Great," said Louie. "Now there are two loonies in this room who are rooting for more crime."

"But what," Chance asked Ted, "makes Sir Tristan's Talisman so important?"

"Sir Tristan was one of King Arthur's top knights."

"Did Arthur trust Tristan?"

"Truly," Ted tendered. "Tristan was a top talent. But Tristan was tormented by terrible temptations, trials, and tribulations which left him torn and tattered, bruised and battered."

"Scarred and scattered," added Chance.

"Twisted and shattered. But one day, Tristan saved the Temple of Twilight from terrifying trolls."

"Tell me more."

"As a reward, the temple priestess treated the trusted and talented Tristan to a truly terrific talisman which Tristan took and tenderly wore around his neck. British teachers tell us that Tristan's Talisman is magical and that no one should tamper with it. Now Tristan's

Talisman is on tour. But the tremendous Talisman was taken from the Tri-City Museum on Tuesday."

"Are there any witnesses?" Chance asked.

"Yes."

"Any clues?"

"Yes."

"Any suspects?"

"Yes."

"Then what's the trouble?"

"I can't solve the case."

"Why not?" Chance asked.

"You'll see," Ted said. "Come downtown with me to the Tri-City Museum and see for yourself."

Chance and Ted drove into an alley behind the Tri-City Museum and got out of the police car. A window was broken, and glass was scattered in the alley.

"Did the alarm go off when the window was broken?" Chance asked.

"No," said Ted.

"Did the security cameras pick up anything?"

"Not at the time of the crime. Someone had shut down the power to the entire building at nine o'clock in the evening."

"Clever," observed Chance.

"But the cameras did pick up this during the day," Ted added.

He walked over to the security television and played some film footage that showed a young woman with dark red hair, dressed in black, walking around the museum. She seemed fascinated with Tristan's Talisman, and she seemed to be looking around for alarms, cameras, and other security measures. In fact, she looked straight into one of the cameras which gave a nearly perfect view of her face.

"That's her!" exclaimed the museum manager excitedly. "That's who I saw break the window and climb into the museum. That's the woman!"

Ted introduced the manager to Chance.

"This is Mr. Johnston. He's been the museum's manager for the past four months," said Ted.

"Pleased to meet you," Chance said while shaking hands with Johnston.

"Likewise," answered Johnston. "I live in an apartment behind the museum. Around nine o'clock on Tuesday evening, I went to the kitchen for a snack. Just then, I saw all the lights in the museum turn off, which I thought was very odd. So I went out on the balcony to take a better look. I saw this woman—the one on the television screen—sneak up to the window, break it, and climb in. I'm sure it was her because I remember her acting suspicious inside the museum on Tuesday afternoon. You don't forget a face like that!"

"Here's a photo of our suspect," Ted said. "Let's go into the next room and interview her."

As they entered the next room, Chance saw a young woman, dressed in black, sitting on the couch, with her legs crossed. She wore a black leather jacket and black leather boots. She even wore a black bow in her dark red hair that perfectly matched the one in the photograph.

Chance walked up to her and asked, "Where were you at nine o'clock on Tuesday night?"

The woman in black gave Police Officer Ted Lincoln a dirty look.

"Who's the twerp?" she asked.

"He's my cousin," replied Ted. "Just answer his questions."

"Ma'am, what's your name?"

"Divinity. Divinity McGinnity."

"Where were you at nine o'clock on Tuesday evening?"

"I was at church," she replied tartly.

"At church?"

"Yeah, I got witnesses! Do you want to talk to them?"

Chance showed her the picture.

"Is this you?" he asked.

"No," she said curtly.

"What do you mean, *no*? How can you deny this is a picture of you at the museum on Tuesday afternoon?"

"Because it's not me, twerp. You must be mistaking me for someone else."

"That's impossible!" Chance insisted.

"Actually, Chance," interrupted Ted, "it's not." Ted opened another door and said, "Come on in, ladies."

In walked two other women who looked and dressed exactly like Divinity. Chance's jaw dropped in surprise.

"Triplets!" he said.

"Now do you see the problem?" asked Ted. "These are Destiny and Trinity McGinnity. They all claim to have been at church at the time of the burglary. Several witnesses verify that they saw *two* of them at church, but they're not sure which two."

Chance looked at the three women. Chance noticed that

Destiny's boots were perfectly polished, that Divinity's jacket had a slight tear on the right sleeve, and that Trinity's eye make-up was a bit smudged.

Ted pulled Chance aside to talk to him privately. As he did, Trinity McGinnity pulled three walnut shells out of her pocket and placed them on the coffee table in front of them. Next, she took a pea out and hid it under one of the shells and quickly mixed the shells around on the table.

"Chance," he said, "we've long suspected that one of the McGinnity sisters is a thief, but we've never been able to prove which one."

Chance watched the women play the shell game. Trinity smiled as she kept fooling her sisters. They could never guess which shell the pea was under.

"Ted," Chance asked, "how does the shell game work?"

"The shell game is really a trick," Ted explained. "The trickster—in this case, Trinity—tries to fool the viewers by distracting them. She tries to get them to look somewhere away from the pea."

Chance thought for a moment. Then his eyes widened as he slapped his forehead.

"Of course!" Chance exclaimed. "The thief is playing the shell game with us! A real pro! And it's so obvious!"

"Do you know who the thief is?"

"Yes! The thief is..."

But at that exact moment, a nearby semi-truck blew its horn really loudly.

HOOOOOOOOOOOOOONK!

Who did Chance say the thief was when the semi-truck so inconveniently interrupted?

(Turn to page 134 for the solution to "The Case of Sir Tristan's Talisman.")

The Case of the Chocolate-Cherry Cheesecake

"I told you the turbo-boost wasn't ready," Lucky Louie said to Chance as he continued to rebuild the engine. "Hand me the straight slot screwdriver."

Chance handed Louie the tool and then went back to staring at the blueprint of the go-cart.

"Well, it's a good thing," Chance said, "that it missed Mr. Hannigan's garden this time. That was close!"

"Yeah," said Louie, "but Heart-Attack Harry wasn't too happy about the new dent in his car."

"He sure gets upset easily," Chance observed. "I sure hope we're not that cranky when we get old and wrinkled. Louie, do you think that we'll ever forget what it's like to be a kid?"

"Nahh! We'll remember what a great time we had. The problem with Mr. Hannigan is that he was *born* old."

The boys laughed. Then Louie's tummy growled.

"Chance, I'm hungry," Louie complained.

"Here. Have another carrot," Chance replied.

Louie stared at the carrots in great disappointment.

"I'm not hungry for carrots," Louie responded. "I'm hungry for ice cream. Doesn't your mother ever buy ice cream?"

"No," explained Chance. "Mom says ice cream doesn't last a day at our house."

"How long do carrots last?"

"Until we throw them out. Look," added Chance as he grabbed one, "this carrot's been around so long that it bends like rubber. On guard!"

Chance handed a carrot to Louie. They faced each other like sword fighters in an old movie, and a mock sword-carrot slap fight broke out. The boys giggled as they ran around the workshop and slapped each other silly.

Suddenly, the tasty sound of an ice cream truck trickled into Chance's workshop. The boys' ears perked up as they dropped their carrots. Chance and Louie leaped to the window; the ice cream truck was still off in the distance, but it was heading their way.

"Money!" exclaimed Louie to Chance. "We need money for the ice cream! Hurry!"

Louie licked his lips as Chance opened the treasury box. Empty.

"Aughhhhhhh!" wailed Louie.

"Quiet, Louie!" Chance snapped.

"I'll cry if I want to," Louie insisted. "Aughhhhhh!"

"No, Louie!" Chance said as he covered Louie's mouth with his hand. "I mean, be quiet. A customer is coming!"

The boys looked out the window. They saw a little girl reading

Chance's detective sign on the workshop door.

"Money!" exclaimed Louie. The sound of the ice cream truck drew nearer. "Hurry, Chance! There's not much time!"

Chance stood up straight and opened the door.

A girl, about six or seven years old, walked in. She was dressed up in a very pretty pink dress and hat, along with white gloves. She was pulling a red wagon with a doll and three stuffed animals sitting in it. They were also dressed up.

"Are you Chase Lincoln?" she asked.

"*Chance* Lincoln," he grimaced. "My name is *Chance*, not *Chase*. I hate being called *Chase*."

"Sorry," she said. "Can you help me? Someone has ruined my tea party."

"Who?"

"Charlie Charter," she answered. "He lives on Chapel Circle."

"And you are...?" asked Chance.

"Oh! I'm Chelsea Cheechy."

"Peachy," Chance commented. "How did Charlie Charter ruin your tea party?"

"I was enjoying my weekly tea with these ladies," Chelsea said as she motioned toward the toys in the wagon. "We form the Chapel Hill Charity. And we were chatting about who to choose for our next charity chairman."

The ice cream truck was getting louder. Chance's mouth watered, and he licked his lips.

"Chelsea, could you please come to the part where Charlie Charter ruined your charity tea? And hurry!"

"Yes, of course, Chase," she said.

"Chance," chirped Chance.

Chelsea continued. "Then Charlie Charter showed up. Charlie said, 'Chelsea, don't you think you should go inside and check on your chili, chowder, and chives?' So I did, and when I came back, our cheddar cheese, chips, and chocolate-cherry cheesecake were gone!"

"That's awful," said Chance.

"Chase..."

"Chance!"

"Chance," continued Chelsea, "can you get Charlie Charter to return our cheddar cheese, chips, and chocolate-cherry cheesecake so the Chapel Hill Charity can choose a new charity chairman?"

"Yes, cheerfully," said Chance. The boys could now see the ice cream truck just outside their window. They needed to hurry. "That will be five dollars, please," Chance concluded.

Chelsea reached into her pink purse and pulled out a fresh, crisp twenty and slid it on the desk toward Chance.

The boys' smiles collapsed as they saw that it was play money from a real estate board game.

Chelsea smiled at them. "Keep the change," she said.

"You're very generous," Chance replied without emotion.

"That's all right," said Chelsea. "There are plenty more where this came from."

"I can only imagine," agreed Chance.

The ice cream truck began to pull away. Louie, desperate, grabbed the play twenty and chased after it.

"When can you begin, Chase?"

"Chance."

"When can you start?" Chelsea asked again.

"Just as soon as I finish my snack," said Chance sadly as he took a bite out of his old, rubbery carrot. It didn't even crunch. He threw the rest of the carrot into the trash. "I'm ready," he said.

Chance looked over the fence into Charlie's backyard. He saw a fourteen-year-old boy playing horseshoes. His tosses were very accurate.

Chance quickly climbed over the fence.

"Are you Charlie Charter?" he asked.

The boy looked at him sharply. "Yeah, and who are you?"

"I'm Chase Lin– *Chance!* I'm *Chance* Lincoln!" he stammered.

"Most people know their own names, stupid! And what are you doing climbing over people's fences?" Charlie snapped.

"And what are *you* doing stealing Chelsea's chocolate-cherry cheesecake?" Chance responded.

"Who's Chelsea?"

"She's the little girl who was having tea with her furry friends when you came sniffing around for free food."

Charlie grabbed Chance by the shirt and pulled a fist back to punch him.

"Why, I ought to..." Charlie snarled.

"I wouldn't do that, Charlie," warned Chance. "My cousin's a cop."

"How do I know that you're not lying?" Charlie steamed.

"Why don't you hit me and find out?" Chance challenged.

Charlie let go of him.

"All right, Chase…"

"Chance!"

"You said your name was *Chase!"* retorted Charlie.

"Yeah," responded Chance. "Well, I made a mistake! We all make mistakes!"

"Well, you've just made one, Chump! I didn't steal anybody's cheesecake. I've never even heard of Chelsea Cheechy before you mentioned her."

"Oh, yes, you have!" Chance battled back. "And if you don't return Chelsea Cheechy's cheddar cheese, chips, and chocolate-cherry cheesecake right away, then I'm going to march into your house and prove to your parents that you did steal them!"

How did Chase–I mean, Chance–know that Charlie stole Chelsea's cheesecake?

*(Turn to page **136** for the solution to "**The Case of the Chocolate-Cherry Cheesecake.**")*

The Case of the Lion with the Diamond

Ted parked his police car in front of Chance's workshop. He saw Chance and Lucky Louie, their faces covered in dirt, pushing their go-cart back to the workshop. It was covered in soil and shredded plants. It was also missing a front wheel.

"Chance, what happened to your go-cart?"

Chance looked up at Ted. "It had steering issues," Chance answered.

"That can happen when a wheel falls off," explained Louie.

"I'll bet," said Ted, as he stared at the skid marks that the go-cart had made into Mr. Hannigan's garden.

The garden looked like a tornado had hit it. All that was left were scattered dirt, shredded plants, and flower petals that were blowing about in the breeze. Deep tire tracks were everywhere, and the missing go-cart wheel lay on top of a bunch of destroyed tulips.

"Chance," Ted asked suspiciously, "*Where* is Mr. Hannigan's garden?"

"All over the neighborhood."

"What happened?"

"Mistakes were made," Chance answered innocently.

"What did Mr. Hannigan have say about all this?"

"Nothing," Chance answered. "Nothing whatsoever."

"Not a word," Louie agreed.

"Why not?" Ted asked suspiciously.

"Because Mr. Hannigan has gone up to that great retirement place in the sky," Chance replied as he and Louie looked up.

"Yes," said Louie. "We miss him already."

"His crankiness."

"His bad attitude."

"His bad breath."

"His bad odor."

"Even his bad music."

"Which he recorded from an elevator because he was too cheap to buy it."

"Yes, Louie, we miss Mr. Hannigan, but he will always be our friend."

"Because everyone needs friends."

"And without us, Heart-Attack Harry would be friendless."

"Amen."

Ted stared at the boys then at the empty rocking chair on Mr. Hannigan's porch in horror.

"You mean, Mr. Hannigan died?"

"No," responded Chance. "He's staying at his vacation apartment on the 70th floor of a skyscraper."

"Mr. Hannigan," Louie added, "said that he desperately needed some peace and quiet."

"So he went to New York City," Chance explained.

"But he's been thinking of us," continued Louie.

"Yes," said Chance. "He even sent us this postcard."

Chance handed Harry Hannigan's postcard to Ted.

The postcard read:

Chance and Louie,
STAY OUT OF MY GARDEN!
–Mr. Hannigan

Ted looked at the postcard, then at the demolished garden, then at the postcard again. Ted shook his head in dismay.

"Chance," continued Ted, "do you remember Mrs. Nellie Nelson?"

"The famous country singer?" Louie interrupted.

"That's *Willie* Nelson!" Chance corrected.

"I thought her name was *Nellie,*" Louie replied.

"Oh, be quiet, Louie!" Ted insisted.

"Yes, from the New York, New York, Musty Museum of Moldy Marvels and Really Old Stuff," Chance answered.

"Exactly. She wants us to go to New York and solve a case for her."

Later that week, after Chance, Ted, and Louie had arrived in New York City, Mrs. Nellie Nelson greeted them near the front of the Musty Museum.

"Thank you for coming," she said.

"Are you going to sing for us?" Louie asked.

"Quiet, Louie," Chance said.

Mrs. Nelson proudly led them through the museum.

Lucky Louie looked around.

"Wow!" he exclaimed. "There sure is a lot of old stuff. What's that over there?"

"That," Nellie said proudly, "is a statue of Plato."

"Who's Plato?" Louie asked Nellie.

"A geek who was Greek," Nellie answered with a smile.

"And that over there?"

"That is a statue of Julius Caesar. It's very old. Don't touch it."

"And what's that old thing that's falling apart over there?"

"That," whispered Chance, "is Mr. Hannigan."

"Oops! Sorry!" Then Louie shouted, "Hi, Mr. Hannigan!"

Mr. Hannigan looked up at the boys in shock.

"No!" he said.

"It's great to see you here!" said Chance. "We got your postcard about your garden a little too late, but we'll help you plant a new one!"

A sudden headache hit Harry Hannigan like a huge, horrible hurricane. "Boys," he said, "you're here. That's impossible!"

"Not at all, Mr. Hannigan!" Chance explained. "You were nice enough to send us a postcard with your return address on it! We plan on visiting you after we're done here."

"My vacation!" Mr. Hannigan said to himself as he fainted.

"Enjoy your nap, Mr. Hannigan!" Louie said happily.

"Night, night," whispered Chance.

Nellie finally brought the group to a large room in the middle of the Musty Museum.

"This," explained Nellie, "is our Mid-Section Collection. It displays our most wonderful and valuable...um...um...what's the word I'm looking for?"

"Artifacts?" Chance chanced.

"Stuff," Nellie concluded.

"Thingies," added Louie.

"Only the finest selections go into the Mid-Section Collection," she said with affection.

"I've no objection," Chance added.

"Each selection has a description inscription that goes through inspections for corrections."

"It sounds like a lot of work," Chance commented.

"It is," Nellie answered, "but the Mid-Section Collection aims for perfection. We display a cross-section of the finest selections that convey a connection with the world's wide recollection. To allow imperfection into our collection would be a distraction from all our attractions. Such an infraction could cause immediate action that would lead to the subtraction of the selection in question. If, upon my inspection, I find an objection, I transfer that selection to the rejection collection."

"Where's that?" asked Louie.

"In the garbage dumpster in the alley," answered Nallie...I mean, Nellie.

"So, what seems to be the problem?" Chance asked.

"Theft!" answered Nellie. "That's the problem! On January eighth, someone stole the Lion with the Diamond! "

"The Lion with the Diamond?"

"Yes," Nellie explained. "It's a small statue of a lion holding a diamond. It was displayed next to the Jaguar with the Sapphire."

"Where were they displayed?" Chance questioned.

"On the floor by the door."

"On the floor by the door? That's a strange way to display. Why not on the table with the label?"

"No, no," insisted Nellie. "We are unable to use the table with the label. The table with the label is old and unstable. If someone thumped, or even bumped, the table that's unstable, then the Jaguar and the Lion would likely go flyin' and smash in a crash—and then they'd be trash. So we set the Lion and the Jaguar on the floor by the door."

"Is there anything more?"

"Yes," Nellie replied. "Only three people have a key–other than me. Here they come. Chance, listen for clues while your Cousin Ted questions them. See if you hear anything unusual."

"Mr. Denver, where were you on January 8th?"

"I was skiing in Colorado," Denver answered. "The snow was like powder. It was perfect."

"Then why is your face sunburned?" asked Ted Lincoln.

"Everyone knows you can get sunburned while skiing, Stupid," retorted Denver.

"How can you get sunburned when the weather's so cold?" Louie asked Chance.

"Quiet, Louie," Chance whispered. "I'm trying to listen."

"I think Denver stole the Lion with the Diamond," said Louie. "I think he's lying about skiing."

"Miss Holly," Ted asked, "where were you on January 8th?"

"I was driving a snowmobile across Australia," said Holly. "I saw all kinds of wildlife you can't find in America. It was cool!"

"Did you see any polar bears?"

"No."

"I think she's guilty!" Louie whispered to Chance. "She's acting too innocent!"

"Quiet, Louie!" Chance said sharply, "or I'll drop a slug down your shirt!"

"Mr. Burk," continued Ted, "where were you on January 8th?"

"I went ice-skating with my niece," the Englishman replied. "Then I took her on a tour of New York. She was very excited. This is the first time she's visited America."

"Do you mind if I speak with your niece to confirm your story?"

"I'm afraid she's already returned home to England."

"How convenient," snapped Ted.

"Not for her," Burk responded. "She had to go back to school. She was very sad."

"He did it!" Louie whispered to Chance. "He made up the story about his niece!"

"Zip it, Louie!" Chance shushed.

Mrs. Nelson leaned toward Chance and whispered, "Chance, do

you have any ideas about who's guilty?"

"Yes, and it is very obvious who stole the Lion with the Diamond," the boy detective replied.

Who stole the Lion with the Diamond?

(Turn to page 138 for the solution to "The Case of the Lion with the Diamond.")

The Case of the Special, Spicy, Spanish Spinach

Lucky Louie sweat as he poured oil into the go-cart engine. He wiped the sweat from his forehead.

"Chance," Louie said, "it's hot in here. Can you open up a window?"

"Sure," said Chance.

As Chance opened the window, he spied a slender, thirteen-year-old girl speedily sprinting up the sidewalk.

"Louie," asked Chance, "did you ever clean up that grease that you spilled on the sidewalk?"

The speeding sprinter slipped on the slick and slammed down with a *splat!*

"Not yet," said Louie. "I'll do it later."

The slim girl stood up on the slippery slick and slid slowly toward the door. She staggered into the workshop.

"Where's Chance Lincoln?" she shouted.

"That's me," Chance smiled.

"You? You're kind of small."

"Yes, but I'm still Chance Lincoln. What's your name?"

"Yes, of course," she said. "My name is Sparkle Spracklin. I just sprinted from the annual Spracklin Spring Spread," she said as she sprayed spit on Chance's face.

"What's the Spracklin Spring Spread?" asked Louie.

"Every spring, the extended Spracklin family gets together for a banquet that we call a 'spread,'" Sparkle explained. "Everyone shows up—Aunt Sally, Cousin Susie, Uncle Spencer…"

"And…?"

"And we feast. We start supper with a simple Caesar salad, followed by super split-pea soup. Then we serve steamy, creamy, squishy, squashy, squelchy squash; sliced, slimy, sour, spring sprouts; and special, spicy, Spanish spinach," she said as she splashed and splattered spittle like a sprinkler. Chance slipped on his safety goggles.

"Yes," said Chance impatiently. "But what happened?"

"Theft!" sobbed Sparkle melodramatically. "That's what happened! Theft!"

"What?" asked Louie. "Did someone steal your plastic spoons?"

"Someone stole all our sprouts, spinach, and squash!" she shouted.

"Did you tell the thief 'thank you'?" laughed Lucky Louie.

Even Chance giggled at that smart aleck remark until Sparkle stared at him sourly. Chance straightened his smile.

"I'm sure stunned that such a stupid stunt should be pulled by someone so shameless as to steal the squishy squash, sour sprouts, and special-spicy-Spanish spinach from the Spracklin Spring Spread," spouted Sparkle.

"Yes, it certainly seems silly," said Chance, his face now soaked. "Louie, hand me your rag."

"But it's all greasy," Louie replied.

"I don't care!" asserted Chance.

"Why is your face so wet?" Sparkle asked cluelessly.

"It's hot in here," Chance answered politely.

"You should get a fan," Sparkle said.

"And a blow dryer," chirped Louie.

"Shut up, Louie!" snapped Chance.

Chance wiped with the dirty rag, smearing grease all over his face and goggles. "Where did everybody go?" he asked blindly.

"Ewww!" Sparkle complained. "That's unsanitary."

"Sorry," said Chance as he put the goggles on top of his head so he could see again. "Where were we?"

"As we were about to sit down to supper and celebrate, someone started the sprinklers," Sparkle said. "So we all sprinted inside."

"Sounds sinister," said Chance. "Any suspects?"

"Sure," she said. "I saw Kimmy Carter sneaking around staring at our spread. When we came out of the house, the squishy squash, sour sprouts, and special-spicy-Spanish spinach were gone. So was Kimmy."

"Seems suspicious," stated Chance as he wiped his face again. Now the rag was soaked.

"Seems *stupid!*" asserted Louie loudly. "Some nut stole your veggies! *WHO CARES?*"

"We care!" insisted Sparkle. "The stealing of our squash, spinach, and sprouts simply spoiled the Spracklin Spring Spread!"

"Why? Do you actually eat your veggies?"

Sparkle stalled slightly. She was speechless.

"That's not the point!" she sputtered. "Someone stole our veggies, and we want them back!"

"So you can eat them?" Louie persisted.

"No, so we can feed them to the pets under the table when nobody's looking! *It's a family tradition!* Besides, Grandma won't serve us dessert until she *thinks* we've eaten our veggies." Then she added, "Chance, can you sniff out the sneak who stole our squash, spinach, and sprouts and spoiled the Spracklin Spring Spread so we can continue our super spring celebration?"

"Certainly," Chance responded. "Where can I find this kid, Kimmy Carter?"

"Kimmy Carter lives kitty corner from us, on the corner of Kitty and Korner."

"Cool!"

"Thanks!" Sparkle said as she paid Chance five dollars. "So long!"

she said as she skipped down the sidewalk until she slipped on the slick spot and slammed down with a *splat!*

"Louie," Chance lectured, "you really ought to clean up that grease slick."

"Yeah," said Louie as he cleaned the engine. "I'll do it later."

Chance saw a small building in the backyard of the Carter house. The sign on the door read, *Kimmy's Klubhouse*.

"Knock, knock," chimed Chance as he knocked on the door.

"Come in," someone said.

Chance entered the clubhouse and saw a fourteen-year-old girl eating at a small table.

"Are you Kimmy Carter?"

"Yeah, shorty," the girl said. "That's me. Who are you?"

"Chance Lincoln," Chance replied. "What's that you're eating?"

"Spinach," Kimmy answered.

"Someone just stole the squishy squash, spicy spinach, and sour sprouts from the Spracklin Spring Spread when the sprinklers sprayed the Spracklin's," Chance said sprightly. "You were seen near the spring spread until all the food was stolen. And now you're eating spinach."

"Look, shorty," Kimmy said sternly. "There were fifty people at that feast, none of whom liked vegetables. One of them probably turned on the sprinkler and then hid the veggies so they wouldn't have to eat them. As for me, I didn't steal anyone's spinach. I went to my uncle's farm, climbed up his trees, and picked this spinach fresh off the branches myself."

"Well," said Chance, "at least you picked the spinach fresh off the Spracklin table."

How did Chance know?

*(Turn to page **140** for the solution to "**The Case of the Special, Spicy, Spanish Spinach.**")*

The Case of the Battered Basketball

"Well, Louie," asked Chance, "what do you think?"

Louie looked over the brightly painted go-cart. It was blue with white trim and had red and orange flames painted on its sides. Louie grinned.

"It's perfect," he said.

"*Almost* perfect," Chance corrected. "It still needs a horn."

"A bright brass horn," Louie added. "Loud enough to wake up the whole neighborhood."

"Yeah," said Chance. "One that goes *ow-OOOOO-guh!*"

"How do you spell *ou-EWWWW-ga?*" asked Louie.

"I've no idea," replied Chance, "What am I? Your English teacher?"

"I hope not," answered Louie, "I've got six overdue essays."

"And you need to know how to spell *ow-OOOOO-guh* so you can finish your essays?"

"No, I just want to know how to spell *ou-EWWWW-ga* in case I want to write it in my journal."

"You have a journal?" Chance asked.

"Of course," answered Louie.

"I didn't know you were literate," Chance teased.

"Drop dead, Chance," retorted Louie, "I lernt too rite in forth grayd."

Harry Hannigan had heard the entire conversation from his rocking chair on his front porch while he was reading his newspaper. He was quietly enjoying the stories about earthquakes, tornadoes, and car accidents—until the boys agreed that they needed a horn loud enough to wake up the whole neighborhood. That sent Harry into a panic. *Reading* about earthquakes was one thing; *living* through them was another. He had to find a way to stop them.

"Where can we find a nice, loud, brass horn?" Louie asked Chance.

Harry Hannigan cringed.

"I know a pawn shop that sells a lot of old stuff," Chance replied. "We'll need our bicycles."

Harry Hannigan watched Chance and Louie ride away on their bikes. Then he stared at the go-cart. It was alone and unguarded. It was parked on the sidewalk which sloped downhill from Chance's workshop to the street below. Harry looked around to make sure no one was looking, and then walked briskly to the go-cart.

"Hmmmm," Harry said to himself as he examined the controls and then looked at the street. "If I unlocked the brake, the go-cart would roll down the sidewalk and into the street. With a little luck, a car would hit it and destroy it. No more go-cart! And it would look like an accident! You're brilliant, Harry!"

Harry grinned as he unlocked the brake. He waited for the go-cart to roll downhill, but it refused to do so. Harry frowned. Maybe the go-cart needed a little help.

Harry went to the back of the go-cart and gave it a good push. It rolled down slowly into the street. A passing truck barely missed hitting it. Then a large car came from another direction and nearly rammed it.

"Come on, come on," Harry mumbled to himself.

"What are you doing?" Louie asked Harry from behind.

Harry nearly had a heart-attack. The boys returned unexpectedly when they realized they had forgotten their money.

"Ah!" Harry yelled in surprise.

"Yeah," added Chance. "What are you doing, Mr. Hannigan?"

Harry panicked. "Nothing! I'm doing nothing!"

"Then why do you have paint all over your hands?" asked Louie suspiciously.

Harry looked at his hands. They were covered in blue paint. He looked at the go-cart. It had his handprints on it. In his obsession to destroy the go-cart, he hadn't noticed that its paint was wet. Panicky, Harry tried to hide the evidence by wiping it on his pants. It didn't do as much good as he had hoped.

Another truck dodged the go-cart. Barely.

"Well, the fact is..." he began.

"Yes?" said Louie.

"Well, I..." Harry stammered.

"Yes?" said Chance.

"The truth is...oh, I can't lie to you boys. The truth is, I pushed your go-cart into the street because I wanted to drive it," he lied.

Chance and Louie smiled ear to ear.

"Well, why didn't you say so?" asked Louie cheerily.

"Yeah," chimed Chance. "All you had to do was ask!"

"Yeah," agreed Louie, "We would have offered to let you drive it, but we thought you hated our go-cart."

"Oh, don't be silly, boys," chuckled Harry. "I *love* your go-cart."

Chance and Louie led Harry to the go-cart in the middle of the street as cars zipped by them.

"What are you doing, boys?" Harry asked.

"We're helping you get into our go-cart," Chance said. "Sit down."

Harry climbed nervously into the go-cart.

"And don't forget to strap on the helmet," Chance added.

"What?" Harry quipped in panic.

"You'll need it," smiled Louie.

Harry broke into a sweat as cars and trucks zipped by him. His eyes widened as he stared at a large, oncoming semi-truck. Terrified, he stomped on the accelerator and turned right and drove up his driveway. He barely dodged the truck, his own car, and his house, but his garden wasn't so lucky.

"My tomatoes!" he yelled. Harry tried to drive out of his garden, but a rear wheel got stuck in the soft soil. In panic, he stomped on the accelerator again. The rear wheels spun rapidly, kicking up dirt and smashing tomatoes all over his windows.

"Wow!" said Louie. "I've never seen so much ketchup in my life!"

The go-cart finally broke free of the garden, along with most of the corn, and crashed safely into the trash cans. Harry staggered out of the go-cart, shaken-up but not seriously hurt.

"COOL!" the boys shouted.

"You were awesome!" Louie laughed.

"Thanks for the drive, boys," said Harry in a daze. "I'll never forget it— no matter how much I try."

"No worries, Mr. Hannigan," chirped Chance. "We recorded everything on our phones! Louie, let's go upload this online so the whole world can see Mr. Hannigan's exciting ride!"

Harry Hannigan collapsed in his rocking chair.

"My life is ruined!" he sighed.

"Sir, can you help us?" Chance asked the big, tough-looking man behind the counter.

The man offered out his huge hand for Chance and Louie to shake.

"My name is Bart Garter. I'm the owner of Bart Garter's Pawn and Barter," the man said good-humoredly.

"What does 'barter' mean?" asked Louie.

"To trade," Garter explained, "without using money. You probably do it all the time."

"Like trading baseball cards with a friend?" asked Louie.

"Exactly!" Garter smiled. "You're very bright. What's your name?"

"Lucky Louie," Louie answered.

"And I'm Chance Lincoln," added Chance.

"Lincoln, eh?" replied Big Bart Garter, "any relation to President Abraham Lincoln?"

"None," answered Chance.

"Oh, that's a shame," said Big Bart, "because I'm about to barter for something owned by Abraham Lincoln when he was a young man. Would you like to watch me work?"

"Sure!" said Chance and Louie.

Just at that moment, Billy Barter, Kimmy Carter, and Charlie Charter walked into Bart Garter's Pawn and Barter.

"It's the Barter-Carter-Charter Gang," whispered Louie to Chance.

"No," quipped Kimmy, over-hearing the whisper. "We're the Barter-Carter-Charter *Partners*, and we're here on legitimate business."

"So beat it, punk!" snarled Billy, the bully.

"I see you kids all know each other," said Bart.

"Yeah," said Louie, "These three are a bunch of..."

"Calm down, everyone," chirped Charlie with a smile. "Leave the past in the past. Chance, you and Louie are welcome to watch while we work. We've got nothing to hide."

Billy Barter pulled a basketball out of his bag and placed it on the counter in front of Big Bart. The basketball was worn slick and made of very old leather. It was signed *Abe Leapin' Lincoln*, in black ink.

"That beauty be a big, bald, brown, battered basketball," barked Bart briskly to Billy Barter.

Billy blinked blankly.

"Wow!" said Lucky Louie loudly. "That basketball is older than my mother!"

"And very, very valuable *if* the signature is real," added Big Bart.

"Oh, it's real, all right," insisted Charlie. "Abe Lincoln was the captain of his high school basketball team. Check the signature. It's real."

Bart pulled out a large magnifying glass and looked over the ball. Next, he opened a notebook and carefully compared the signature on the basketball to a real signature of Abraham Lincoln. Bart's eyes widened as he whistled.

"It's a perfect match," he announced.

Charlie began the negotiations. "The Barter-Carter-Charter Partners wish to barter with Bart Garter. Mr. Bart Garter, what is your barter starter?"

"I'll start with two go-carts, and a cart of tarts," bartered Bart.

"That's a slow starter, Mr. Garter. Maybe the Barter-Carter-Charter Partners should be smarter and barter with another barterer," said Charlie Charter.

"Okay, okay," Bart Garter re-started. "I'll throw in some art, an ox cart, and a photo signed by Bogart."

Charlie smiled slyly as he turned to the others. "Let's depart and leave Bart," he said. Barter, Carter, and Charter started for the door.

"No, wait!" said Bart. "I'll throw in three *gold* darts!"

"Gold darts?" Kimmy Carter remarked with a spark.

"Yes, but that's my *final* offer!"

"It's a deal!" Charlie announced as he stretched out his hand for a deal-clenching handshake.

"Just a moment," interrupted Chance. He quickly whispered something to Big Bart. Big Bart's eyes widened with surprised anger as he slammed his giant fist onto the counter top with a *boom!*

"I've got a better deal," Big Bart bellowed. "Take your worthless ball and get out of here, and I won't call the cops!"

What did Chance whisper?

*(Turn to page **141** for the solution to "**The Case of the Battered Basketball**.")*

Epilogue

Harry Hannigan couldn't handle it anymore. He looked out his upstairs window and saw Chance and Louie with the monster they called their go-cart. They were laughing as they took turns gunning the engine and crashing into his trash cans. The noise was horrible. The mess was worse.

When Harry was a kid, he didn't waste his time with go-carts. Instead, he grabbed his fishing rod and ran off to a nearby stream.

Why couldn't Chance and Louie be like him and quietly go fishing in a nearby stream far, far away?

He watched them as they slammed into his trash cans again. Harry began to get a splitting headache. If only he could get rid of their stupid go-cart!

Then an idea hit him.

Harry raced to his bedroom safe and opened it. He pulled out a large sum of money. Then he went to the front porch and called the boys to him.

"Oh, boys!" Harry called out, more singing than talking.

"Yes, Mr. Hannigan?" they answered.

"Boys, it's a hot day, isn't it?"

"It sure is," replied Chance.

"How would you boys like to buy yourselves some ice cream?"

"Yeah!" they both shouted gleefully.

"I'll tell you what, boys," Hannigan said as he waved his money at them. "I'll buy your go-cart from you, and then you'll have enough money for ice cream."

"I don't know," said Chance. "We really like our go-cart."

"How much will you pay us for it?" Louie asked.

Harry grinned maliciously. "One thousand dollars."

"A thousand dollars?" the boys yelled.

"That's a lot of ice cream!" Louie added.

"Are you sure, Mr. Hannigan?" Chance questioned. "I don't think it's worth anything close to a thousand dollars."

Hannigan clenched his teeth as he spoke. "Oh, believe me, boys. It's worth every penny! Buying this go-cart from you is going to make me the happiest man on Earth!"

The boys looked at each other and then at Mr. Hannigan.

"It's a deal!" they cheered.

The boys took the money and chased down a passing ice cream truck.

Mr. Hannigan could barely contain his laughter as he pushed the go-cart into his backyard.

Later that day, Chance and Louie stuck their heads over Mr. Hannigan's backyard fence.

"Hi, Mr. Hannigan. Are you having a barbeque?"

"I *had* a barbeque, boys," Hannigan smiled as he sprayed water onto a pile of wet, steaming embers. "I'm just finishing."

"Did you have hot dogs and hamburgers, Mr. Hannigan?" Louie asked.

"No, boys," laughed Hannigan. "The black ashes you're looking at are all that remains of your awful go-cart. I'm sorry, but I bought it fair and square, so I can do anything I want with it. It's nothing personal."

"Oh, we don't mind," Louie said. "After all, it's *your* go-cart."

"Sure," added Chance. "Well, have a nice day."

"I will, boys. I will," Hannigan said happily as he nodded his head in agreement. "I thought they'd be in tears," Hannigan said to himself. "I guess those boys aren't so bad after all."

Hannigan turned off the hose and started walking toward his house. It was time to sit quietly, enjoy a good book, and then doze off to sleep. It was time for some peace and quiet.

All of a sudden, he heard the sound of a hammer.

"Ow! Watch what you're doing, Louie!" Hannigan heard Chance yell from Chance's backyard.

"Sorry," Louie replied. "It was an accident."

"Give me the hammer," Chance demanded. "This time *you* hold the nail!"

Hannigan looked over the fence in horror. The boys were hammering some nails into wood.

"Please, don't miss," pleaded Louie.

"Don't worry," Chance said as he brought the hammer back for a mighty blow. "I never miss."

"Chance!" Mr. Hannigan called, "what are you boys doing?"

"Oh! Hi, Mr. Hannigan!" replied a surprised Chance as he slammed the hammer down.

"Ow!" shouted Lucky Louie. "Just kidding! You missed me!"

"We're building a new go-cart with the money you gave us!" Chance said excitedly.

"Yeah, thanks to all that money," Louie added, "we bought more powerful tools!"

"And a bigger engine for the go-cart!"

"And a louder horn!"

"And an awesome music system with powerful speakers!"

"And, deep, deep bass that sounds like an earthquake!"

"And big, thick tires that really kick up a lot of dirt!"

"My garden!" said Hannigan as he slapped his forehead, fainted, and fell to the ground.

Chance and Louie stared at Hannigan lying on the ground.

"Is he all right?" asked Louie.

"He's fine, Louie," replied Chance. "He's just taking a nap. He must have been so happy that he couldn't stand the excitement."

<u>The End</u>

<u>Solution:</u>

<u>The Case of the Jewelry Janitor</u>

Chance knew that Mr. Motley was lying about seeing the janitor steal jewelry because neither he nor Ted could see through the reflecting windows when the inside lights were off.

Mr. Motley confessed to stealing Ms. Jazmyn's jewelry, and Janitor Jenkins became the new store manager.

*(Turn to page **14** to read the next case.)*

Solution:

The Case of the Purple Puppies

Chance knew that Pippy made up the story of her trip to Antarctica when she claimed she saw polar bears. Polar bears only live on the opposite side of the world in and near the Arctic Circle. They have never lived in Antarctica.

Pippy confessed that she stole the pack of purple puppies and hid them in her pappy's penthouse in Pittsburgh, Pennsylvania.

(Turn to page 23 to read the next case.)

Solution:

The Case of the Silver Caesar

Chance knew the coin was a fake when he read "45 B.C." "45 B.C." stands for "45 years Before Christ," meaning before Jesus Christ was born.

First of all, the Romans had no idea that Christ would be born forty-five years after the coin was made. Secondly, nobody used the term "B.C." until hundreds of years after Christ was born. And finally, "Before Christ" are English words. The Romans didn't speak English; they spoke Latin. The English language did not even exist in 45 B.C.

The Sosser brothers confessed that they made the fake coin and then pretended to find it while diving for seashells. As a punishment, their parents made Shel and Seymour scrub ship floors by the seashore.

*(Turn to page **35** to read the next case.)*

Solution:

The Case of the Buttermilk Biscuits

Chance knew that Billy Barter made up the story of trading Matt the Bat when he noticed that the bat's cage had feathers in it. Only birds have feathers. Bats are mammals, and, even though they fly, they do not have feathers.

Billy Barter gave back Betty Baxter's butter, berries, batter, and biscuits. Betty was so happy that she let Chance buy three buttered, buttermilk biscuits for three cents during a thirty-second sale.

*(Turn to page **48** to read the next case.)*

Solution: The Case of Sir Tristan's Talisman

"The thief is Mr. Johnston!" Chance remembered that the glass from the broken window was scattered in the alley. But Mr. Johnston claimed that he saw one of the McGinnity sisters break the window from outside. If the window had been broken from outside the museum, then the force of the blow would have pushed the broken glass inside the museum. But someone inside had smashed the window, which drove the pieces of glass into the alley. Someone who is *already* inside the museum doesn't need to break a window to get in.

Chance realized that Mr. Johnston had stolen the Talisman and then had broken the window to make it look like a burglar had done it. He then attempted to blame one of the McGinnity sisters for his crime.

Ted and Chance later learned that Mr. Johnston had worked at several other museums for short periods of time. Each had been robbed during the time that he was its manager.

(Turn to page 62 to read the next case.)

Solution:

The Case of the Chocolate-Cherry Cheesecake

Chance knew that Charlie Charter had stolen the cheesecake when Charlie said that he didn't know who Chelsea was but later mentioned Chelsea's last name. The only reason for Charlie to lie was to hide his crime.

Charlie Charter returned the cheesecake, and the Chapel Hill Charity elected Chelsea Cheechy their new charity chairman. To celebrate her victory, Chelsea gave Chance and Louie half of her chocolate-cherry cheesecake. The boys cheered as they chewed.

(Turn to page 75 to read the next case.)

Solution:

The Case of the Lion with the Diamond

Chance knew that Miss Holly had stolen the Lion with the Diamond when she said that she was driving a snowmobile across Australia on January 8th. While January 8th is during winter in the Northern Hemisphere, it is summertime in Australia. Miss Holly could not have driven her snowmobile across Australia during the summer.

Miss Holly returned the Lion with the Diamond, which was placed between the Jaguar with the

Sapphire and the Geek who was Greek.

*(Turn to page **91** to read the next case.)*

Solution:

The Case of the Special, Spicy, Spanish Spinach

Chance knew that Kimmy Carter stole the squishy squash; sour sprouts; and special, spicy, Spanish spinach when she said that she climbed trees to pick spinach. Spinach doesn't grow on trees. It grows on the ground.

Kimmy Carter returned the stolen veggies, much to the despair and distress of the Spracklin's, especially after Grandma Spracklin locked up the pets. However, Grandma was so thrilled about Kimmy loving her veggies that she invited Kimmy to join them for dinner. The Spracklin's welcomed Kimmy to supper and then secretly slipped her their squishy squash, sour sprouts, and spicy spinach. Then Grandma served the Spracklin's scones and snow cones for dessert.

(Turn to page 102 to read the next case.)

Solution:

The Case of the Battered Basketball

Chance whispered, "Abraham Lincoln died in 1865. Basketball wasn't invented until 1892."

The Barter-Carter-Charter partners got smarter and fled Bart Garter's Pawn and Barter.

As a reward, Big Bart gave Chance and Louie a big, beautiful, brass horn that could (and did) wake up the whole neighborhood–along with a photo signed by Bogart.

By the time the boys got home, Mr. Hannigan's exciting go-cart ride had been viewed by ten million people.

Not the End

*(To finish reading **Chance Lincoln, Boy Detective**, please turn to page 118 to read the "**Epilogue**.")*